Number 42

WILLIAM DOUGLAS

First published in 2022 by Tortive Lit.
Tortive Lit is a part of Tortive Theatre Ltd.
The Straw Yard, The Barracks, Parade, Berwick-upon-Tweed, TD15 1DF

admin@tortivetheatre.com
www.tortivetheatre.com

ISBN: 978-1-7396920-0-1

INTRODUCTION

On the 12th December 2015 a body of a 60 – 70-year-old man was found on the Chew Track from Dovestone Reservoir in the Peak District National Park. The man was lying down and appeared to be resting with his arms across his chest. When Detectives arrived at the scene, they suspected that he had not died of natural causes. Detective Sergeant John Coleman saw the body and said;

"It appeared to me that the male had sat down and had taken the conscious decision to lie backwards."

Only the following items were found on this man's body.

- £130 in £10 notes.
- Train tickets for his final journey
- An empty medicine bottle emblazoned with Arabic writing.

There was no form of ID, no mobile phone, no bank cards, no credit cards, or anything that can be used to identify him. He was the forty-second unidentified body found in the UK in 2015.

At the time this play was first produced, in early 2017, the identity of the man remained a mystery. Later that year the body was finally identified as former London Underground Tube Driver, David Lytton.

There is no factual evidence that the events as written in this play ever occurred. It is merely a story inspired by the discovery of David Lytton's body and the mystery surrounding it. No disrespect is intended to the family or friends of David Lytton.

FIRST PERFORMANCE & PRODUCTION

Number 42 was first produced by the Worcester Repertory Company at the Swan Theatre in Worcester from the 21st - 25th February 2017 with the following cast and crew.

The Woman
Victoria Lucie

The Man
Jonathan Darby

Director
Chris Jaeger

Lighting and Sound Design
Jack Coleman

* * *

CHARACTERS

The Woman

The Woman is intended to be considerably younger than The Man but could be played by a female actor of any playing age between 26 - 55. She is highly intelligent and before we see her change at the end of the play, she has a puppy-dog-like, endearing demeanour. After we see the shift, she becomes very 'matter of fact', not 'evil villain'.

The Man

Ex-military, and highly intelligent. He has a warm demeanour to him, and a worldly authority gained through experience. The intended age of the man is early 60s, but this could be flexible. The part of the man could also be played by a female actor if considered appropriate to the production.

There is no inference made by the author as to the race of either of the characters.

* * *

PRODUCTION

The play is designed to be staged in the simplest way possible and could be produced with nothing but a bench. Set and lighting can always be built into the piece depending on budget and resources. It is a short play and is perfectly suited to one-act play festivals and scratch night.

If the procurement of a replica firearm (as required on page 17) is problematic, please feel free to cut that part. It is not integral to either the plot or the characters. Please feel free to do this without reference or permission from the author or the agency. Similarly, if any of the coarse language (although there's nothing too horrendous in there) proves problematic, then feel free to remove as needed.

CONTENTS

NUMBER 42

The side of a hill near Dove Stone Reservoir. On the stage there is a bench and nothing much else around. Lights fade up and eventually a man enters. He is in his sixties. He is wearing a pair of comfy slip on shoes corduroy trousers, shirt, sweater and a jacket. He is not dressed to be on the hill. He looks ordinary but out of place. He has a Marks & Spencer's bag with him. He sits on the bench and takes out a sandwich, opens the packet and eats. After he has finished he puts the sandwich packet back in the bag and places it beside him. He takes in the scenery around him and is content. After some time a woman joins him. She looks out of breath, as if she's been walking for a while. She has a rucksack and is dressed for any situation the hillside may throw at her.

Woman
Afternoon.

Man
Afternoon.

Woman
Good day for it, isn't it?

Man
For what?

The woman looks at her own clothes.

Woman

(Jokingly) For swimming. For walking on the moors. Beautiful views around here.

Man

You're not wrong.

Woman

Do you mind if I…

She indicates that she'd like to sit down. The man makes a token gesture of moving up slightly. She takes off her rucksack and puts it down in front of her as she sits next to him.

Woman

I've not been up here before.

Man

Really?

Woman

Nope. Not really a massive walker to be honest. But this is just stunning. A bit chilly though. Aren't you cold?

The man simply shrugs.

Woman

Do you know, I might do more of this? Walking, taking in the scenery. It's so peaceful here. Nothing to bother you at all, is there?

The man simply looks at her.

Man

Nothing at all.

Woman
Sorry. I suppose you want to be left alone, don't you?

Man
Why would you say that?

Woman
Well, you're sat on a bench in the middle of a national park, not really dressed for the part and you're looking wistfully into the distance. It screams solitude if you ask me.

Man
Well, once again, you're not wrong.

Woman
Right. I'll be quiet then.

The woman goes into her rucksack and pulls out a sandwich box. She sits and eats, all the time irritating the man next to her. She then pulls out a bottle of water and takes a loud slurp. Again, this irritates the man. She then goes into the bag a third time and takes out a packet of crisps. She starts to eat them and gradually becomes aware that the man is now very fed up with her presence. Her eating slows and she offers him a crisp. He simply looks at her and she sheepishly removes the packet and places them back in her bag. She zips up the bag and places it in between her legs. She breathes in deeply. The man has now had enough.

Man
Do you mind?

Woman
Sorry. I was just trying to enjoy the peace and quiet.

Man
As was I.

Woman
Well, excuse me for breathing. Literally.

Silence

Man
It's a lot of money.

Woman
Pardon?

Man
I said, "It's a lot of money."

Woman
What is?

Man
What you've spent on all that gear. For someone who's not a massive walker, you've spent a lot of money on all the right stuff. Brand new walking boots. They've not seen the rain. That jacket's worth a couple of hundred quid, and the rucksack's almost as much. That's a lot of money to be spending on equipment when you're not a walker.

He looks at her. She's not really sure how to react. The game is up for her.

Woman
Shit.

Man
You can spot you new ones a mile off, you know?

Woman
I thought I was doing really well.

Man
Don't be so hard on yourself. We've all been there. You try and get your first one right, down to the last detail and you end up going overboard. I did exactly the same.

Woman
Oh balls. I thought I'd got it all right. I had a whole script worked out and everything.

Man
Sometimes you can plan too much. They don't teach you that in training. Sometimes you just have to go with it. So I take it I'm your first then?

She nods.

Man
You're very different to the rest of them I've seen.

Woman
What do you mean?

Man
You seem normal.

Woman
Aren't we meant to seem normal?

Man
Yes. But I can imagine you having a family, husband, two point four kids. That sort of thing.

Woman
Oh god no. I think that's why I did so well in the army to be honest. Nothing to hold me back.

Man
Army, eh? Same.

Woman
Which regiment?

Man
Paras. Then Hereford. Fairly traditional really. You?

Woman
Intelligence Corps.

Man
A sneaky beaky hey? Do you know we used to say that the only thing you lot were good for was curing insomnia and colouring maps?

Woman
Yes. I got a lot of that.

Man
Doesn't matter anymore now though, does it? You don't exist.

Woman
Neither do you.

Man
Well, I do for a bit longer. Maybe not on paper, but I'm still breathing. For just a little bit longer.

Pause

Woman
I'm…

Man
Don't. That's yours. Don't give that to anyone.

Woman
(*Indignantly.*) How do you know I was going to tell you my real name?

Man
Because you don't think it matters. You think that because I'll be dead soon and you're the one that's got to do it that it gives us some sort of bond. You think that you can afford to let it slip this once, just because I'm an old hand at this and who I'm I going to tell?

Woman
How do you know that?

Man
Because I've been where you are. I've done all this. I've made the same mistakes.

Silence.

Man
You were, weren't you?

Woman
Maybe.

Man
Give me a false name.

Woman
Natasha.

Man
Hello Natasha. I'm Neil.

Woman
Really?

He looks at her again.

Man

Christ. They send you. Of all people, they send you. How does that work, eh?

Woman

Excuse me. This is hard.

Man

I know.

Woman

Oh. Yeah. Of course. Sorry.

Silence.

Woman

Why here?

Man

Why the moors?

Woman

Yeah. Of all the places you could have chosen to go, why here?

Man

Because this is where my first one was.

Woman

Oh. I see.

Man

I just thought it would be neat. Complete some sort of transcendent circle. I thought that it would allow a small glimmer of justice in this whole stupid thing.

Woman

Do you regret it?

Man
What, my first one?

Woman
All of them.

Man
There's nothing to regret really, is there? It's our job. We kill people.

Woman
So, you've no regrets then?

Man
Do you regret killing anyone you've killed?

Woman
(Flippantly.) Well, I've not done one yet have I?

The man shoots her a look.

Woman
Sorry. I mean. I've pushed buttons. Given the 'operational go-ahead'. That's killed people. But I've never done one face to face. Not like this.

Man
It's different.

Woman
So they keep telling us.

Man
It never goes away. The face of someone who's life you've taken. It's there. Always. I can still remember being here. I can remember the smells, sounds, the look of fear in his eyes. The fear that turned

to peace. There was something quite beautiful in that moment. It made me feel…feel…

Woman
Okay about it?

Man
God no. How could you ever feel okay about it? But I did feel nothing. Well not nothing. It was more a feeling of neutrality. Something that needed to happen. I didn't feel okay about it, but I didn't feel bad about it either.

Silence.

Man
It's funny. I asked the same question.

Woman
What question?

Man
Why he'd chosen here.

Woman
Oh, God, it wasn't his first one as well, was it? I'm not going to be part of some never-ending death loop.

Man
No. He had a much better reason. There was a plane that crashed here in the 40s. He was on it with his parents. They both died but he survived, somehow. He had no family at all, so he became a ward of the state. The government got their claws into him when he was a kid and they never let go. Quite sad really. He was young. Well, younger than I am. He was in his early 40s, if that. I was about 26. But because he'd been at it so long his end had come early. So, he decided to come back here, where his parents died. I think it was the only place he really felt connected to. I didn't really appreciate that until recently. When the whole wind-down started, I thought, "where do I want to go?". I hadn't got a single

connection. Not to a place. Not to a person…a time. So, I chose here. It seemed like a defining moment. The only one. The one I couldn't come back from.

Silence.

Man
(Trying to wind her up) And for my full circle, my transcendent moment, they sent you.

She smiles.

Woman
Why do they make us do this?

Man
How do you mean?

Woman
To one of our own? This would be so much easier if it were an enemy of the state or a drug lord. God knows there are plenty that need getting rid of. Why do we have to do this to one of our own?

Man
Well, the purpose is twofold. Firstly, they don't want it to be easy for you. They want it to be hard. As hard as they can possibly make it. You've heard the old spook joke about the recruitment process?

She shakes her head.

Man
Well, three recruits for a government agency not too dissimilar from ours were down to their final test. They were each presented with a gun and a door. They were told that to pass the test they had to walk into the room and put a bullet through the head of whoever was on the other side. The first recruit walked in and saw his wife. He couldn't do it. Couldn't even raise the gun to point it at her. So, he failed. The next recruit walked into the room and saw *his* wife. He got a little further. He managed to point the gun. But he just couldn't pull the trigger. So, he failed as well. The last

recruit happened to be a woman. She walked through the door and saw her husband tied to the chair. On the other side of the door the assessing agents listened eagerly. They heard the shot of the gun and then a lot of commotion, and things being thrown all over the place. After about five minutes the recruit comes out of the room covered in blood and says, "The gun you gave me had blanks in it. So, I had to beat the bastard to death with it instead."

The woman is not sure how to take this. The man finds it very funny.

Woman
That's a bit sexist, don't you think?

Man
What, to suggest that the woman would have been better at the job?

Woman
No. To suggest that the women cared less about her other half.

Man
How would *you* know?

The woman doesn't give anything away, but just stares at him.

Man
Sorry. That was insensitive. The point is, that they don't want to make it easy on you. They need to know you can do the job.

Woman
It makes sense, I suppose. What's the other reason?

Man
Sorry?

Woman

You said that there were two reasons.

Man

Ah, yes. Well, the second one is simple. How shall I put this? 'Turnover of Staff'. You see, you can't have old spooks like me walking around all over the shop. It's not that we're a risk. But what happens if we get dementia or through no fault of our own start revealing state secrets? You can't really have that now. So, it dovetails quite nicely into a training exercise for you and clean-up operation for them.

Woman

Well…we're nothing if not efficient.

Silence

Man

So, what's on the menu then?

The woman goes into her back and rummages around.

Woman

Well, I prepared a number of things dependent upon who you were. *(She pulls out a gun.)* I brought this. That was if you became a bit volatile. Just thought I do it quickly. *(She pulls out a knife.)* This if we were going to be in a busy place. First one just between the ribs to stop you screaming and the second one bringing it round to the femoral artery. *(She pulls out a syringe.)* This is if I found you sleeping. No point in waking you.

Man

(Sincerely.) That's thoughtful, thank you.

Woman

See…women do care. And then I brought these. *(She pulls out a bottle of pills.)* I thought I'd give you the option…you know…if you wanted to do it yourself.

The man takes the bottle and examines it.

Man

Good god. Where did you get this stuff? I haven't seen this in years.

Woman

Pakistan. Routine intelligence gathering. Nothing special. Training camps, that sort of thing. Our CO took those of us who were out in the field aside and mentioned this stuff. Not as quick as cyanide but does the job and much easier to find. You can buy it over the counter over there. I've always kept it with me, just in case.

Man

You know it won't count?

Woman

I did wonder.

Man

You have to do it, I'm afraid. They have to know you can do the job, remember.

Woman

That's fair enough.

Man

Besides, I've been doing this for over thirty years. I really don't think I should be expected to have to do my own as well. I think that goes a bit far.

Woman

It happens though, doesn't it?

Man
What does?

Woman
People like us. They can't cope and they just end it.

Man
Yes, they do. There are only three ways for one of us to go. By the hand of our enemies, by our own hand, or by our replacement's hand.

Woman
It makes you wonder whether it's all worth it.

Man
What? The job? God, I was well into it before I started asking those sorts of questions.

Woman
Did you not miss any of the normal stuff? You know, kids, wife, normal job?

Man
It was never there to miss. Was it?

Woman
No, I suppose not.

Man
So, why none of that for you then? Why none of the 'normal' stuff?

Woman
It just never really happened.

Man
Did you want it to happen?

Woman

I think I did at one point. Not a huge fan of kids to be honest but it would have been nice to find someone. But then the test results came back. You know those ones that they say are "routine psychological evaluation questions." But they're not. They are testing to see who's got it in them. Who could be a killer; to see who could do this job. And then you don't think anything more about it, do you? You go through training, start doing your job, start enjoying the life…

Man

And then someone like me comes and offers you something a bit different.

Woman

"We've been following your career for some time, and we think you've got something different about you. Something that could be very useful to this country." They don't mention at that point that the 'something' different is the same thing that used to keep you awake at night when you were a teenager. That it's the same thing that meant you had to fake tears at your own grandmother's funeral so that people wouldn't think you were weird. That the 'difference' in you is why you don't feel what other people feel; why you don't feel what you *should* feel. No…you find that out later.

Man

So, why did you say yes then?

Woman

(Mockingly.) I'm a woman. Sometimes I like to be told I'm special.

Man

Isn't that a bit sexist?

Woman

It was the money.

Man
Oh yes, the money.

Woman
I mean it was silly. I'd have had to get to Brigadier before I was earning that amount of money in the Army. But then you think about it. What's it for? I mean how much of it have you spent?

Man
Not much at all.

Woman
So, what's the point? I mean it's not like we can leave it to anyone, is it? We haven't got anyone to leave it to.

Man
I've left mine to charity. The Dog's Trust. All coming in from different names over the next ten years.

Woman
That's nice.

Silence.

Man
I'm not sure you really want to do this.

Woman
I'm not either. But it's a bit late now, isn't it? As you said, there's only three ways I can go.

Man
There is a way out…if you wanted it.

Woman
Really?

Man
Yeah. It's not commonly done, but if you really don't want to go down this route you don't have to. There is a way of backing out.

Woman
Well, what is it?

Man
You take all my money, disappear, and start a new life. It's not as if you can't. They've trained you to do it.

Woman
They'll come looking for me.

Man
Not if I do it to myself. They'll just think that you've lost your bottle, got cold feet about the whole thing and disappeared. As long as you don't start drawing attention to yourself, they'll leave you be.

Woman
How do you know?

Man
Because it's what my first told me, and I've seen it happen.

Silence.

Man
There is a part of me that wishes I'd taken him up on the offer, to be honest with you.

Woman
Why didn't you?

Man
I was young. Wanted the excitement, the adventure, the paycheck.

Silence

Woman
Would you come with me?

Man
No. I can't.

Woman
Why not?

Man
Because then they really would come looking for you. And I need to do this. There's no place in the world for people like me. The world always thinks it needs heroes. But just occasionally it needs monsters, and I'm afraid that monsters don't get happy endings. No. I need to complete my transcendent circle. It's right. It's proper.

Woman
That's what we are, isn't it? Monsters.

Man
The world needs us to be, sometimes. There are people too dangerous to be kept alive and if people like us didn't do what needed to be done then think of all those people who would get to meet the other monsters. The monsters that don't keep them safe.

Woman
When I was a little girl I didn't grow up thinking that I was going to be a monster.

Man
You're not one yet though, are you? You can just walk away.

Silence.

Woman
Would you do it differently?

Man
What?

Woman
When your first told you about the way out. If you had your time again, would you take the way out?

Man
But I don't have my time again, do I? My story is finished. Yours has barely begun. Whatever happens now, this is my spot. This is where I stop being a monster. I have done terrible things. I have done things that have turned me into the monster I was there to stop. But it ends here, today. Just like my first

The woman looks at him with a mixture of pity and unease.

Man
You don't have to worry about me. It's what we sign up for. You know that. One day you'll have to pick your spot. You'll have to choose the point at which you're no longer a monster. But once you've got to that point, you can't be anything else. So, the monster will have to go.

Woman
I'm not sure I want to be a monster.

Man
I don't think you do. But for what it's worth, you'd have been great at it.

Woman
Would I?

Man

Yes. You're the only one of us I've ever met that was able to irritate someone enough to make them want to top themselves.

They share a smile.

Man

Look, I can't tell you what to do with your life but you don't have to do this.

Woman

I can't make you do yourself though.

Man

Why not? It seems only right, thinking about it. I can stop with my circle right here. You don't need to carry it on. Quite literally 'end the cycle of violence'. But you have to do everything else, okay? All the things they told you that you must collect. You need to do that. Otherwise, they will come for you.

The woman thinks about this for a moment. She's made up her mind.

Woman

Okay then.

She goes to her rucksack and takes out a piece of paper.

Man

Oh, bloody hell. What's that?

Woman

My list.

Man

Your list? I take it back; you're piss-useless at this.

Woman

I just wanted to make sure I didn't miss anything.

Man

Jesus. Go on then.

The woman also takes out a plastic back and then goes through her list. As she calls out the items, he puts them into the bag.

Woman

Right. IDs. Any jewellery including watches. Credit and Bank Cards.

Man

You'll be needing those. You know how to access them?

The woman nods.

Woman

Any weapons you might be carrying on you.

Man

Nope. Nothing.

Woman

What, nothing at all?

Man

Well, I could give you a nasty paper cut with my train tickets, but I think I'll keep those on me.

Woman

Why?

Man

It will confuse the hell out of the police and the press. They'll spend ages trying to work out who I am. I even brought a return ticket. It was only a pound more expensive than a single.

Woman
Okay then. Anything else?

Man
Just this.

He hands her the Marks and Spencer bag with his sandwich rubbish in.

Woman
What's this?

Man
It's my rubbish.

Woman
What?

Man
I don't want my last act on this planet to be littering, do I? What if a sheep or something came past and started chomping on it? I've told you…here's where I stop being a monster.

Woman
Well, thank God the wildlife of the moors can finally rest easy.

Man
Is that everything off your list?

The women double checks.

Woman
Yep. That's it.

Silence.

Woman
You'll be number forty-two, you know.

Man
Forty-two?

Woman
You'll be the forty-second unidentified body found this year. I checked on the database. They were up to forty-one just before I came up here.

Man
Well, hopefully they'll find me quickly. I don't want to be forty-three. Besides, *The Hitchhiker's Guide to the Galaxy* is one of my favourite books.

Woman
Hey?

Man
Number forty-two? The meaning of life? Doesn't matter. I wonder how many of those forty-one will be monsters like us. Sorry. Like me.

Silence.

The woman reaches in her bag and pulls out the bottle of pills.

Woman
You'll want these.

She places them next to him and looks forward.

Woman
Do you want a drink or anything?

Man
No thanks. I'll be alright.

He takes the bottle of pills and stands up. He looks around and finds a spot.
He sits down and opens the bottle of pills.

Woman
What are you doing?

Man
Lying down. I don't want to go sat up like that. I'll end up falling
off the bench or something. If I'm on the ground I can look up at
the sky. Such a beautiful night. How long do these take?

Woman
My CO said about thirty seconds to a minute until you can't move
and then a couple of minutes until you're asleep.

Man
Thank you.

Woman
Would you…like me to stay?

Man
No. You've done your part.

The woman goes to leave. She stops.

Woman
Just so you know, my name is Natasha.

Man
I know.

Woman
How?

Man
I told you. You're piss-useless at this.

He smiles at her. She smiles back.

Woman
Yeah. I am.

Man
Natasha. You're not a monster. You never were. Take care.

The woman leaves and the man takes a couple of the pills and lies down.

The lights dim slightly. After about 20 seconds the Woman re-enters, she sits and looks at him.

Woman
It's not Natasha.

Man
W-what?

The woman's following speech should not be played as 'evil villain' but as matter of fact.

Woman
Sorry. You see, I'm not useless at this at all. I'm really very good. Shooting someone? That's easy. Stabbing them is a little harder, but still not really that difficult, is it? Needle? Well, that's the easiest of them all. But this? Now this is really creative. All the gear I had on, the list, the story about how I ended up here, my name…all a set-up. You see killing someone is easy. But convincing someone to kill themselves? Now, that is a real challenge. I've always known I was a monster. I've always known that the world needed people like you and me. But there's a difference between us. I quite enjoy it. I didn't like the fact that I enjoyed it at first. But that finger on the button. The power. The feeling of control. Nothing quite like it.

But now I've done this, there's no going back on it. It just feels right.

The man lets out a little laugh.

Woman
What's funny?

Man
(Struggling to speak) I'm actually quite proud of you.

Pause

Woman
I wish I could say that meant something. But I don't feel it.

Woman gets up to go.

Woman
I'm a monster.

She exits.

As the lights fade the man struggles to say his final words.

Man
I am not a monster, anymore. I am not a monster anymore; I am not a monster…

Light's fade to black.

ABOUT THE AUTHOR

William is a drama school graduate and holds an MA in Creative Writing. He has written several plays for young people as well as, full-length and one-act plays, articles, short stories, and commissions.

As a professional director he has directed and produced shows all over the word and continues to work as a consultant to theatre companies and organisations throughout the UK.
He lives in Scotland with his wife and children.

NUMBER 42

www.ingramcontent.com/pod-product-compliance
Lightning Source LLC
Chambersburg PA
CBHW061321140726
47998CB00006B/2493